AMERICANS, GUESTS, OR US

AMERICANS, GUESTS, OR US

CAREN BEILIN

NEW MICHIGAN PRESS
TUCSON, ARIZONA

NEW MICHIGAN PRESS

DEPT OF ENGLISH, P. O. BOX 210067

UNIVERSITY OF ARIZONA

TUCSON, AZ 85721-0067

<http://newmichiganpress.com/nmp>

Orders and queries to nmp@thediagram.com.

ISBN 978-1-934832-37-0. FIRST PRINTING.

Printed in the United States of America.

Design by Ander Monson.

Cover art by Jesse Bercowetz.

CONTENTS

Our Orchard   1

Ballet's Bullets   2

Siblings   6

Mysterious Visits   8

Your Darker Dot   9

Zoo Balloons   11

Where to Find Things   14

The Naming Incident   15

Living Together   16

Letter Left on Counter   17

The Argyle Eagle   18

Home Remedy   21

Surgeries   22

Problems Outdoors   23

Death Balloons   26

Awkward Gathering   27

The Activity of Love   28

Linens!   31

Secret Folded Letter   32

Natural History   33

From a Pig's Mouth   34

Ourstory   36

Animals are Placebos   37

Why You Can't Follow, If You Can't   39

Night Appetite   40
Bound to Happen   41

Acknowledgments   45

for Dee, for telling me to find the fawn

OUR ORCHARD

There is a moon orchard where small growing moons
are becoming panoramic in width, against black string
grass, attached to vines that are underground connected
to something. To birds. If you see a bird as a bird it is:
wing, breast, flush, its singing, its phrasings (above the
grass) calling forth itself in reverse, so that if a bird were
a photograph this were its negative, in a different dress
of color, the titillating opposite or hollow of the color of
the other, and together they go into the darkroom which
is night, its lamps fixed over many chemicals. But if you
treat a bird as a seed not a bird and plant it and let it
blow, from its hollow, buried bones balloons of moons,
then here is our moon orchard. The moons are many,
the orchard is long. They are hot white squash, round
and rock, light vermilion fuzz on it, if vermilionness
were populous incandescence, everywhere. If you go out
with me to examine the vines, to touch them with your
sensitive handskin, they are coated in the underfur of
feather, that gray spritely moss you have seen beneath
and around a colored feather of a bird. If you touch one
of the many moons in our orchard, they are cold and
oozing freezing dew. If you put your ear near enough:
the soliloquent echo of a bird sputtering her used
instinct (for mating) through a twinkling vine, into the
heartrock of Earth's outer space.

BALLET'S BULLETS

I am taking a ballet class even though I am not flexible or social. I show up at the studio armed, just in case, but the bags, anyway, stay in the locker room. My leg doesn't make it to the barre and they wheel in a lower barre for people like me. The teacher is the kind of American who tells herself she's French. Je, she says, instead of I, mixing up who she is by mixing up where she is. We are in America. There is a Chevrolet illegally parked outside. Nobody's grandfather was in the Legion.

Nobody else uses the low barre and it gets in everyone's way, just a little bit, just enough to make them hate me, and shame tingles on every single part of my body, it even tingles on my clitoris, I can feel it, and this, unfortunately, turns me on, because shame is often part of my sexual routine. So I start having pre-orgasmic pangs, little bells dinging and waves rushing over the dinging bells. I love ballet class.

After class, my teacher comes up to me and says, "Don't worry about the low barre. It didn't bother anyone at all." She says it as though she just ate Brie and is about to drink noontime wine, that I've interrupted her at her French table, that I was walking down the Place Du Champ and I came up to her and disturbed her—an American tourist—and she said, "Don't worry about the low barre. It didn't bother anyone at all."

I'm not used to talking to people so I shrug and say
I'll be back next week and then we'll see. In the locker
room, I put my clothes on over my leotard and one of
the other women says, "Didn't you sweat?"

"You don't sweat as much when you use the low barre."

"It didn't bother us at all," she says. She puts her head at
a tilt to signify she's comforting me.

I go home and masturbate away all of the built up
shame. It's a bunch of butterflies in my expanded clitoris
that I grind into orange monarch dust against the
mattress, my mortar. I love ballet class. In the middle
of the night, I break out into tears. I am not, just not,
a dancer, I think. I sit wildly up in the bed and try to
touch my toes, and what I'm surprised about is that I
haven't worn holes into my clitoris yet.

I stretch and stretch all week, masturbating more and
more and then less and less as I begin to be able to
touch something: my toes. I take the bullets out of my
gun.

And in the next week, yes, I do not need the low barre at
all! I need, if anything, a higher barre. "Do these barres
go any higher?" I ask.

4

"No," our teacher says. But it sounds like *Non*. Actually, it sounds like *Fuck you*.

In the locker room, I take off my leotard and my tights and put on my pants and my shirt. The other women look impressed by my social graces. Or, they look less annoyed, more neutral, less tilted. I go home and hardly have to come at all. I do it lazily, working on a vaginal orgasm for variety, and I feel a small beep and go to sleep.

I feel so smug all week that I don't stretch at all, and again, again!, I need the low barre, which is so humiliating, and shame comes in a sludge, a mucus whorl that feels too thick to masturbate away. I have to fantasize the whole class about gun violence, even though I was so confident I didn't even pack today, and so confident I'm not even wearing tights, which I realize, looking in the mandatory mirror, are always necessary no matter who you are. Your flesh hangs out and jiggles. Anything but this. Anything but the low barre after the high barre, life, with its aching ups and downs. Its holy highs and low blows.

I switch to photography classes in the same building, which come with a 24 hour dark room pass. Nobody can see your face, let alone the outline of your labia—

thank god!! Much better!! I go down the hall to my old ballet class and, with permission from someone, shoot everyone. I shoot our French teacher, and the women who taunted me in the locker room. I shoot myself in the mirror shooting them. I'm the class drop-out who comes back with a vengeance. In a dark room, I think about all I've done.

SIBLINGS

Children were gutting the least popular child's pet turtle
on the street, its shell put to the pavement, its guts soft,
accessible by butter knife. I told them to stop, in a moral
tone, and they did, they sulked away, leaving me, Adult,
in charge of clean-up. None of the kids were related to
each other. There are a lot of only-children living on our
cul-de-circle so they call us China because of it.

The fortunate thing was that in the gutting of the
turtle, there were lots of turtle eggs exposed that with
care and basic know-how would hatch. We just had
to build a simulated turtle womb, which I reasoned
correctly would be an instructive project for all the
children involved in the slaying, and could perhaps serve
as a curative for the turtle's young, picked-on owner, a
solution to death and also, a way to make friends.

We did it at my house, in the mud room. There was
green goo everywhere, and lots of packed needles
in nitrate boxes that came from abroad-based
labs—scientists we wrote to in a humble tone seemed
to smile down at our activity and we even received
congratulatory notes on our commendable actions
which we framed and hanged as part of our project. I'm
instilling pride, I went around—the lawn, the trees, the
living room—thinking. I did other things thinking only
this.

The children, you could really tell, looked down with envy at the eggs, which vibrated in the self-amassing ball of green goo, the expanding makeshift womb, the chemicals that we injected into a basic kitchen solution. They were all only-children and their egos were worked on by all of these siblings, the thousands. They expressed their feelings of loneliness and their fears of being the sole caretaker for aging parents, of turning out a homosexual disappointment—all that you would expect.

"Oh," I said, "don't worry about that now."

We all reached in together and touched tenderly the green goo.

"And besides," I said, "when these are hatched, there will be so many of them that it won't matter if you kill some of them."

MYSTERIOUS VISITS

We were walking and then you went inside a house
that I had no idea you knew. I didn't know you knew
the people in that house. You came out when the moon
had risen, a bird's eye view of a cup of electric milk.
How do you know those people, I asked. I don't, you
said, I'm just more social than you, more easy about life.
The people came out and sat on their porch and waved.
They looked sinister.

YOUR DARKER DOT

There was a summer not long ago if you count the
entirety of natural history, if you consider the black arch
of eons, when I tried to make a map of the frogs that
inhabited your parent's lake. But this isn't about them.

On the map, the lake was a square the exact size of the
piece of paper it was drawn onto and the frogs were
idiot green dots. The dots were placed all around the
lake, some in social clumps and some on their own,
the way I must be seen from space, and there was no
emaciated breeze, and no unbearable sun, as I remember
the sun to be. I did not include your tongue on this map,
even though I certainly remember your tongue to have
been in this lake. I remember it in the lake, and in my
mouth, the softest of pink sandwiches.

Your breasts are not on the map, either. They would
have been a couple of beige dots, each with an inner,
darker dot. The two beige dots would be just slightly
larger in circumference than the perhaps thousands of
green dots.

But at the time, I remember, I wanted all of my maps to
have one subject each. I felt very strongly about this—a
map of clouds that excluded birds, a map of fish that
cartographered no bank, no hooks or line, not a

person's knees as he waits, or his hungry belief in death. I mapped your parent's bathtub once by dipping a piece of your firm stationary into its hot water, those swirling roads of foam.

You said, "Why not include me in your map of the lake, since here I am in the lake, naked as a skinned apple?"

"This is only going to be a map of frogs. You know that's how I work."

Of course, I was the true naïf, since the frogs moved around, would not stay put (they are a patternless animal, not dogs, not beavers, and not anything whipped to be a way, you cannot whip one) and I should have mapped your breasts, their dots, since, looking back, that is what I wish to remember, and what I wish to find my way back to.

ZOO BALLOONS

At the zoo you can buy animal balloons, dead birds on
strings given shots of helium into the rectum and they
jounce overhead attached by the string for an hour.

I joked that I wanted a lion balloon but there actually
were lion balloons, but most astounding, we saw a
buffalo balloon, held on a string by the littlest girl whose
parents held only clutches of bird balloons, red robins
and blue jays over their heads in bouquets of balloons,
but birds, tugging them down so that they bobbed up.

Children always do the same thing with a balloon
which is to release it across a cloud. They don't think
of pollution or that river animals will choke on the
excess of their spectacle, for time itself is an excess of a
spectacle. Time sits like fat at the gate.

It is not surprising that the littlest child of all the
zoo—it was awkward that she wasn't an infant, it
seemed so recent, and time had really bullied this frail,
vein-compiled thing out of a papoose so soon—released
the largest, most spectacular balloon, the completed,
inflated, helium-blooded buffalo over the zoo where it
bobbed into the clouds never quite becoming nothing
the way regular rubber balloons squint into tiny dots.

Children love the release of a balloon. They don't
understand how helium works, though I remember I
understood and would cherish the death of my balloons
in the living room as they incremented into the rug and
the whole house took on the air of hospice and I stroked
the balloon where it wrinkled and began my path to
intuitive understanding that to inject it with air would
be to kill it, that the very nature of injection—pin,
plunge—was in opposition to the nature of balloonskin,
that there was no solution, no transfusion, though the
ingredient for its survival was everywhere, was air.

But these clever zoo animal balloons were not so clever
since animals have holes, orifice and pore, fuckslots
and things smaller than fuckslots, holes as varied as
professional pebbles or the American monetary system.
So it's not as if the animal balloons could last long at all.
They were only upward for moments before people like
this littlest girl's parents dragged only clusters of birds at
their feet, like walking a molting, dead, abstracted dog, if
a dog abstracts into birds.

The buffalo, due to and against the size of its body, went
far into the clouds, bobbing against the under tufts of
their curving fluffiness, a body buoyant even with its
rugged ancient look, even its horns filled with helium,
the bone teeming with elation, so that it rammed into
the clouds, parting them, with puppetry, and what is a

balloon but a drugged puppet but an elated, perverted marionette?

The buffalo parted one cloud over the zoo and everyone watched with a sense that it had all been planned, that reaction would be inappropriate in the context of a zoo, in the context of cages.

I used to name my balloons as they died on our living room rug, dignifying their death with a life and saving their withers like colorful stretchy ashes.

I named this buffalo secretly in my head, standing next to you, as it descended again onto our zoo, there being no wind. I named it for the little girl whose name I did not know, and people were not surprised when her buffalo balloon landed in a cage for Antarctic animals, its pores and anus wheezing out helium on an incongruous island of ice.

It was felt—the way you can feel that you all feel—by everyone, that these animals wouldn't know how to use this buffalo which was now too heavy to be ever removed. It's a shame, it was unanimously felt, that this particular balloon didn't land in a cage for lions because they would know exactly what to do or the Native Americans you could tell we were all slyly thinking.

WHERE TO FIND THINGS

We keep our cleaning chemicals—bleach, stain-remover, Windex—in the refrigerator for preservation. We are committed to preservation.

THE NAMING INCIDENT

You named a star for me behind your wife's back and
here is the certificate, and I feel that you expect me
to hang it in my kitchen proudly like a diploma I just
got. It's not that much of an accomplishment to have
your name up there. I spied on you last night and you
walked out with your wife with a basket and the two
of you were picking down stars like the night was your
personal romantic orchard. They did not burn the
basket or turn into glitterless rocks. If we went star
picking, I'm sure our stars would not be the same, if you
look at the fate of my life, or if you picked the one with
my name on it, it would be rotten. We'd try to pretend it
was just as firm as the other stars, but it would be a star
rotten in its core, and the basket would sigh and like a
dog beg us to go home, which means we'd part, and it
would abhor the stars as though they were sour crumbs,
disgusting bright bread it had to carry.

I saw you with your wife. Her gown blending its
organza ruffles into a wild flood of good rabbits.

LIVING TOGETHER

Take heart, I am leaving, will leave you first. I have ropes and snacks, am prepared, have pumps. I don't have a lot of friends. When I have left before I have not gone to their houses or the houses of friends who once were. I used to have access to these houses but a cut friendship cuts a rope that cuts me off from the key to these places besides bushes, these places the cars on the street seem to be smelling.

I will not go to friends' houses, having none.

At some point, I did. I did begin to think of my friends as their houses, this network of sheltering, this web of roofs. Which is when I started to despise my friends and love you. With you, I could live in a bush. We could live in your car.

But then, you want this bed, this meal, and a life, and appliances, which suggest that things aren't ok the way they are but need to be conveniently differentiated. Appliances are chambers for transformations, they are electric betterment closets.

I want to remain a solid. Your blender is such a violent cunt.

LETTER LEFT ON COUNTER

Prioritize the rooms that you clean in our house. We are
in dire need of dusting, and the trash smells rotting, as if
somebody lit melons on fire, though that's not it. There
are food stains on everything in the kitchen, food is like
ink. The carpets go next. We make a real effort around
here not to drink on our carpets, but the occasional
loose drink splatters, our hands occasionally jolt out of
control, and some of our guests' muscles have diseases.
The pink you may notice, like an exploded tongue,
flecked unfortunately, is blood we tried to bleach. See
what you can do. There are dove rags draped over the
oven door.

Don't go into either of our studies or the room that is
farthest from the guest kitchenette, but please get to
that kitchenette. In the master bedroom, clean without
opening. Have a no-opening mindset. Do not open
our drawers or our closets, our containers or the cages.
Do not open boxes in the storage pod no matter how
alarming their labels. If you do end up using bleach as
the primary curative for stains, keep the windows up.
Wash the windows with Windex. Don't use Febreze on
even stinking furniture. It doesn't work.

If you are tired, take a light break. If you are done, the
money is under the Buddha.

THE ARGYLE EAGLE

There is an argyle eagle in the shed, but now it's hopped out of it and sits on the small roof. It is the kind of shed that appears like a small house, a young house if houses grew. Gray and blue diamonds fall into neat interlocking rows on the argyle eagle's wings and there is an isolated diamond on its head, but it is not footwear. Not even close!

We go up to it because a) we're bored and b) it's rare and fantastic, the kind of thing you'd want to touch if only on the top of its clutching claw, if you stand on your toes next to our shed.

"Hi there," we say, sounding neighborly. It creeps its eyes into the sun. Its irises are not in the shape of diamonds. This, if anything, is where the pattern breaks, two glowering circles.

Eagles have been known to fell great-sized trees, redwoods, so there is a part of us that wants to shoo it off the shed, as much as we really want to make it stay. There is a trapping part of us, a packing part.

"You there," we say, which is not very neighborly sounding, much more accusatory, like policemen finding lingering kids, or blacks.

We don't know where it came from, or how it'll go back.
It doesn't look at us at all. It doesn't do anything. It is
statuesque except that its wings go calmly up and down,
as though this needs to happen. The wing-underneaths
have no diamonds. They are shockingly red. We jump
back.

"I've never jumped back because of a color before," I tell
you. And you look at me very warmly, with that look
that says we've built this life together but here you are,
surprising me with a new aspect. And I want to fuck
you, after a month of not wanting to fuck you. I want to
fuck you in the shed with the argyle eagle on top of it.

I think that's why couples like us, out here, here-ing it,
get small-house sheds. We want a little fuck room. We
want to go into our small house and do everything very
differently, the shrunken, emboldened versions of our
large selves. All the tools hanging still.

We go inside of it, through the door looking like a
house door, and this makes the argyle eagle look briefly
down at us. I just wish it would go away now. I wish
it would lift off and never come back. The whole time
we're in the shed, that I'm fucking you differently than I
do in the big house—I put my scrotum on your open

eye and command you to blink rapidly, something I've always wanted to ask, "Look at me five hundred times, you cunt,"—I can't help but be concerned we're going to collapse.

HOME REMEDY

Tears dissolve superglue, but if you cannot cry (you've
already cried and you aren't going to cry again), make
an animal cry and use that, if you have connected two
objects—cup to table, desk to bed, tree to house—and
now they seem miserable together, unacceptably
connected, the connection was a mistake, a mistrial.
Make the animal—the rabbit if possible, something
domestic, a dog—cry however you see fit. Use tools
or emotional factors. Put the dropper (poise it) up to
the animal's eye with one hand and have your tools (or
factors) in the other. Apply. Disconnect the things that
should not be connected forever.

SURGERIES

Will you switch coronaries with me? I have one of each of my parents' kidneys. An ex-lover and I switched livers on our anniversary (I won't tell you how many years, but it was many, and it was brutal, and it was bitter) and my friend (the one I kept from childhood, that one) has a pure gallon of my blood and I have some of his, and my lungs are two robins, their wings numbed and severed prior to insertion, so my breath cycles through their hollow bones.

A coronary works in any body, if both bodies are alive and the coronary is healthy, if it is a glowing fist. It is a matter only of opening ourselves. I am confident that it would work, that one of us would not reject the other's organ, that one of us would not hold on and the other not, for naught (they'd say). That one of us would not have the pain of carrying the other person's last part, the punctuation that did not die though the sentence did die. That.

I have confidence in our medical team, in the way the hospital corresponds to my dreams of hospitals, the waxed floors, when I close my eyes, waning. I am so positive that we, together, will breathe again.

PROBLEMS OUTDOORS

Our secret sex is out of control. Last night I came over
while your wife was in bed and we had it in the den,
the door not even completely closed, ajar. I did not ring
the bell but rather slipped in through your open garage,
which gaped at me from down the street, or, from across
the cul-de-sac. I went into your mud room, your living
room, to you, our hands together, then, us, the den.
Your wife was asleep with the television tuned to the
elections, which are a compendium of polls thrust into
the froth of choice. Her neck was exposed. I saw. Like a
child being allowed to look in on a corpse.

We did it in the den, the old couch, your graduate
couch, though you did not graduate. Neither did I.
We're two losers which is part of the gratification
received through the channels of our fuckery.

You put a tweed pillow on my face so I wouldn't wake
her up. You tied a velvet wrapping ribbon around my
throat to turn me on. We dumb types like to get turned
on by S/M, by out of the ordinary, by doggery, dogged
fuckery. We enjoy scraping our skin on tweed, while
someone, her, sleeps, her brain in a dream, her moon
rolled over onto its dark part.

But while we were fucking it became apparent that
a fawn was watching, a young deer twitching by the
computer chair, shivering in the central conditioning.
It was almost lower than us. Its nose came up to our
connecting, frantic (feral) groins.

"This is not like a bird in the house," I groaned.

"Shh," You said. "Her."

Fawns are often outside. They cross the road in rows, or
they stand in the middle of our cul-de-circle or in the
evening try to gather on the deck. If the doorbell rings
and no one is there, a fawn's body has brushed against
it, but then went away. If there is air at the door, and not
you. Or not me.

"What shall we do with it?" I said. I began to put on my
clothes, pack up my cunt.

"Shut the fuck up," you pleaded, referring to your wife.
Who, we both knew, would know what to do.

You walked past the fawn who stood so stiff, its ears so
up. Your penis was down, as though someone stabbed
it with an injection of Ambien. You opened the door
and made prophetic motions. I put on my final sock. I
unwrapped my neck.

It ran into her room, that door open too (why are we so reckless, why do we want catching, like children falling from trees?). It butted against her bed (your bed). It put its nose, which had seen our groins, on her polite face, those cheeks you chose.

When she woke up, she knew what to do, you told me today, you reported the news into my receptive nipple: "She very calmly led it to the mud room, using an animal knowledge I do not know. She wasn't even fully awake. Sometimes I think her dreams must be smarter, more logical, more with sense, than my waking life. She once told me she writes books in her dreams, that this is where she crafts ideas. To be that cognizant, when you are not. To hold onto your life, when I have so easily slipped out of my life."

Into my other nipple, your teeth bared, biting and talking: "But in the mud room, there were at least eight more, all huddled under the coats, like escapees, war stowaways, their noses tucked into our shoes, a scene. And my wife said the smartest thing. She said—"

And into my cunt, you echoed: "What must be wrong out there?"

DEATH BALLOONS

We make balloons out of the dead. We put helium in the corpse and tie a string around the foot, and there you are, with that person bobbing above you. If you are a child, release it into the clouds where it will twinkle into a dot and adults will pollution-bemoan you, sure, but they'll say besides, you are having fun, and besides you are a mourner.

If you are an adult, with a dead child for a balloon, hold onto it, until it wrinkles into a wither on your living room floor, for a while static against the wall and then almost as if sitting upright like a child on the couch, and then a colorful shrivel on the rug.

If blood is still dripping from the balloons, take heart, for a balloon can only bleed air, its air not shepherded out from any lungs.

I have seen children put pins in other children's balloons, on the sly, at the zoo, or at home, between brothers. I have seen them save the rubber in piles, eclectically colored corpses, and I have seen humans pile other humans, having used their lungs like balloons, and pinning their loins with gun-pins.

AWKWARD GATHERING

What is my role with a grieving friend? She is
coming to my house within one hour and I am in the
kitchen—spoons, stove—wondering how to expose my
receptors, getting nervous. What could she want from
me? What are the things I will say to her, what needle
will I prop up to her brain and what serum of comfort
could I possibly inject, in this twisted nursing scenario?
Nervously, I stuff a bird with plums, ginger, and sugar
and put it in a covered pan.

When she comes over, it is as though she doesn't
have eyes anymore, or they are squinting with frantic
emotion or when they are open they are empty, the
pupils, the irises in hiding, or covered in a fog of milk,
and she isn't asking what smells good, what's in the pan,
my curative dish. I am a private person. I would never
do this to her. I would not show up at her house. I scoop
plums from the bird's womb and put them in a personal
bowl. I would not behave like this, refusing hot plums,
asking instead for alcoholic tea.

I would not position myself so psychologically naïve. I
wouldn't go to someone, since I know that when we are
weak, we are susceptible to torture.

THE ACTIVITY OF LOVE

If you do an activity, wear the clothing of that
activity. Do not show up in a priest's outfit (if it isn't a
priesthood) and do not wear any percentage of cotton if
the requirement of the activity is to sweat. Don't wear a
hat if a hat is not intrinsic to the activity at hand, if the
sun is not somehow involved, if it is night.

Everything on your person should be about what you
are doing. For instance, if you are playing tennis in the
evening, you should wear the gear of a tennis player and
nothing else. Not jewelry: opal, gold, silver, ruby, metal,
et al. Do not wear even a plain watch or a heart monitor
or lipstick. Don't soak your underwear in champagne in
the morning, before you play tennis at night.

If you are making love, if you are a coital clone of your
neighbor's wife, (she is a myth for a series of moments,
an inside joke, an imagination, a laughable sphinx), do
it with your clothes (your pleats) off. Put your pleats
on the railing if he is going to enter you, and have him
do the same with his pleats. From a distance (you are
distant, your brain is distant) they look like two stacks
of plain business envelopes.

Only use your body parts. Leave props, for once, out of
it, since props come in between bodies, even when

the props are designed to connect those bodies, those
people, you two. Don't use a scent on yourself. Let the
scent—whatever it is, groinal, lion saliva—come from
within.

Focus only on the activity. Use your hand if inspiration
lubricates its bones. Touch him on the neck. You are
the kind of lovers who use necks—you both threaten to
cut off air, to choke for fun, since choking corresponds
to your genitals. Take your shoes off if you haven't yet.
Throw them in the direction of the trees. Let slugs oil
them with their excrement while you are connecting
against the net (your naked ass is divided into squares,
someone could come up and draw a chart on it, could
track the changes that you can't).

Now that it is over, look at him through the thatch
of one of the tennis rackets. Tell him something
sentimental through it—you love him, you hate
this—and kiss him through the tightened strings like a
conjugal visit.

If you tear up, only use tears. If you get dressed, only use
clothes. Walk around the court getting them. If you are
ashamed and you are dressing, do not use leaves, since
you are not Her. He isn't Him. If his wife appears in

your brain, a chemical that feels acidic in the cerebellum
(did angels jab that needle full of it in? did they fly down
in their ragged tennis clothes?) wear the soul of a fawn
and flee.

LINENS!

If you sweat on the sheets then skin them from the bed and leave them in a bilious clump for us to deal with when you're finally gone. Don't sweat on or near our sheets if you can at last help it. The fibers will begin to think they belong to you, and not us. We will charge you. We will want our sheets back if you take them from us. Returned in full. We threaten daily.

If we find you have left your smell, the smell your heart makes when it's juiced by a dream, on our sheets, we will kill you with elbows we've pickled into knives in the barrel of nighttime.

SECRET FOLDED LETTER

You left your underwear in the Kleenex box and guess
who pulled it from its puffed position to blow her nose?
We were sitting in the sunroom making phone calls
and doing anonymous, vicious acts, and then she had to
blow her nose and then I saw that she held your delicate
underwear in her hands, that she emptied snot into the
crotch area, balled the whole small thing up and threw it
out, into the rotting waste bin between our feet.

Don't leave your underwear here ever again. I had
to masturbate in the mudroom several times in the
middle of the night, thinking of her nose touching the
daguerreotype of your cunt, the oily footprint.

You are like fucking a deer in that it seems so
impossible. It seems that your inner-nature would have
shot you out into the night. It seems that your blood
would have told you that you were not safe if found.

NATURAL HISTORY

I am sitting here with a bottle of lotion, masturbating.
I don't think of fantasies when I do it. For me,
masturbation is all about the sensation of my genitals
and I don't need to invent holograms in my head. I
don't need to construct dioramas of sexual situations,
our bodies—mine and yours—taxidermied, our skin
stuffed, me fucking you a certain titillating way, your
stuffed breasts in my stuffed fingers, a prop bed beside
us because we have taken it to the prop floor, your sweat
made of glue-drops. My glass eye.

FROM A PIG'S MOUTH

Where did you go last night? I was looking for you everywhere in my mind. I thought of all the places you could possibly be, the different houses you tend to visit, those of people you've always known. I never got up out of bed. I didn't call out the window. I just trembled in the bed thinking, Where is he? Where is he now? Where could he be? I didn't even check to see if the car was gone. I wasn't really looking for you. I was (more) looking for my thoughts of you. I thought of you and then tried to understand the thought, like instigating an illness to study a greater disease, which doctors do. They do.

I heard you getting up after midnight. I heard, in the bathroom, the shower charging over your body, the bristled water. I heard you shave. I heard the razor speak on your chin. I pretended to be in a haze of a dream, which got me wandering, How many people here, we here-ing it, are pretending to dream at this moment? I felt guilty, for all of us. I started to think of what my dream might be, going into the subconscious backwards, or wearing it inverted. I was conscious. My hand was steady.

I thought I would dream of pigs. Everybody always thinks they'll dream of something like that, that if

pigs have anything to say to us, they'll say it when we
sleep. But really, when we really close our eyes, when
we aren't awakened because you are in some form or
another walking out, we don't think at all about pigs and
their pink position in this world. We don't do slovenly
translation work. I don't know much about what we do
but this we don't do. Not much.

You left. You didn't touch my skin before you left. It was
dark outside. Your shoes were on.

I can't tell you what I forced the pigs to tell me, in my
forced dream I forced myself to have even though I was
very much awake, like shoving a pig through a sieve. I
can't tell you the rotten things this pig told me about
you.

OURSTORY

You reintroduced me to yourself under the pretense
that we remembered each other but forgot names, but
you used a new name. Your new name was much worse
than your old name, which rhymed with a popular
ancient bird so much that to call it out was to sing in
another language. I called it out, in your arms, and you
carried yourself imperial and inhuman and divinized
as if you were the moon but couldn't confess it, and it
was so curious that I always saw you during the day, and
had never heard of your name before. Now, your name
is much more human and American. I ran into you at
night, with a woman, and you seemed to be drinking
again. I told you the same name as I had then, but you
looked surprised by it, as if you remembered something
so strange. You looked at the ground impatiently as
though I used to be a bird.

ANIMALS ARE PLACEBOS

Animals are placebos. Take a rabbit to feel better. Rub
dove balm on your throat at night. Eat dog. There's
nothing better to take, when there is no medicine to
take, no science to ingest, no pill that clamps a clock on
a nerve, winds it backwards toward increased flexibility,
mobility.

There is an incurable disease, and I say take an animal.
Take it softly by spoon. Chew on its tail in the bath, or
turn it into butter, churn it.

If you can't cure your disease, if the doctors say you can't
walk, if they say your nerves have broken their feet, and
your spine has been stripped of its protective gelatin, if
one of your systems went dark and there is no cure, hold
an animal at the cave of your mouth. Put a rabbit in. Put
a turtle in.

If they tell you that science is slim and the world is
puffing off of it with ease, like an out of control yeast,
walk out of the hospital, but do so slowly. You'll have to
do so slowly.

But once the right number of animals have been taken,
possibly rare animals, animals from the bottom of the
ocean, their brains ancient, their hearts as simplistic

as boxes, you will notice an improved mobility, an improved spinal capacity. You will bend and run, coming out from one room into another. Take a bird with pleated wings and use an appliance on it, juice it. Drink sweet, light bird juice.

If your hands stutter over the checks you write, and your muscles jump involuntarily, and you can feel the flesh in your thighs sparking out, use animals as placebos. Take them at night, clutch their fluttering bodies to yourself in the bed, or put their ears on your tongue, and wait, with false, effective hope.

WHY YOU CAN'T FOLLOW, IF YOU CAN'T

I have been making maps again that nobody thinks
don't point to schizophrenia, and this is because the
maps lead to nothing, or something unintelligible. I
have thought that the problem is the basement and
if I worked on my maps in the kitchen or on the
computer they might become acceptable, somehow,
even publishable. Not sick maps. But I make them in
the basement and come up smelling of the exhaust of
bushes. I know I have a messy hand, as though its bones
have been mangled by a mangled mind. But I tell you
this: I map in the basement to keep myself moving. If
you can't recognize the places that I am drawing (and
going to), it is because you own a house, built from the
bricks of slaughtered bushes. It's because you've got your
house like stars in your eyes that you can't see other
places, in my mind.

NIGHT APPETITE

If you are naked, get dressed. I am dressed. I am wearing sequin butterflies over each breast to bed each night. We have the heart of a stallion on the counter that we keep out, cured, and shave slices off, like Spaniards with their pigs. But our appetite is stronger than this heart and I eat yours. I eat it through your naked sequins.

BOUND TO HAPPEN

Your wife caught us because she has nothing else to do.
Her function bleated before us in the bedroom: a wife
is a catching mechanism. The baby was in her arms.
A baby really does have nothing to do as it spins in its
inundations of everything.

We inundated the baby, your dick in my mouth, my
cunt apart, the pillow full of birds.

The baby, in its inundation of everything, was not
surprised, not even by the birds, for he, at the time of
this writing even, has not seen enough birds to know
by virtue of pattern that birds don't belong stuffed in
a pillow, wingless as rodents, a wing in your mouth, a
wing taped over my mouth, a wing on my crotch like
Eve's leave, and wings on the sheets like torn pages from
a bird-bound book. A baby cannot understand yet that
something looks romantic.

Your wife, who I have seen sleeping before, her tongue
a black-caressed pink, now held her mouth open and
screamed.

You took your dick from the hole in the wing over my
mouth. I spoke through the fuckhole in the wing, said,

"Scoot! Fly, fly away, you whore." Nobody expected that. Babies don't expect, or need, much.

The baby was crying but only because babies are crying. There was no dog. There was no dog barking. This was in the early evening when the cul-de-circle gets rust in the grass as though the grass grows old and the deer move in like a school of fish, crowding on our decks tendon to tendon like slaves roaring to America. They have that determination. Your wife must have waded through the deer on your and her deck to get to us, stepping over all the wild blood only to know this about our blood.

ACKNOWLEDGMENTS

Pieces from *Americans, Guests, or Us* have appeared in *DIAGRAM*, *Big Lucks*, *Everyday Genius*, *Pear Noir*, *Jerry Magazine*, *Left Facing Bird*, *Torpedo*, *Open Letters*, *elimae*, *Corduroy Mountian*, and *New River*. A grateful thank you to those editors and readers.

And special thank you to Brandon Shimoda and Lisa Schumaier, early encouragers of these pieces in particular.

CAREN BEILIN has published her fiction in *McSweeney's, Fence,* and *The Lifted Brow.* She is from Philadelphia and currently lives in Salt Lake City as a student of creative writing.

❧ ☙

COLOPHON

Text is set in a digital version of Jenson, designed by Robert Slimbach in 1996, and based on the work of punchcutter, printer, and publisher Nicolas Jenson. The titles are in Futura.

NEW MICHIGAN PRESS, based in Tucson, Arizona, prints poetry and prose chapbooks, especially work that transcends traditional genre. Together with DIAGRAM, NMP sponsors a yearly chapbook competition.

DIAGRAM, a journal of text, art, and schematic, is published bimonthly at THEDIAGRAM.COM. Periodic print anthologies are available from the New Michigan Press at NEWMICHIGANPRESS.COM/NMP.

CPSIA information can be obtained at www.ICGtesting.com
Printed in the USA
LVOW10s1627140914

404005LV00005B/500/P